Waterlogged

CLAIRE SAXBY

Illustrated by Sue O'Loughlin

sundance™
A Haights Cross Communications Company

The Characters

Josie

Dad

Steve

Lena

Carlo

The Story Setting

picnic area

to the water-ski area

Home Cove

swimming

boat ramp

beach

to parking

snack bar

to city

3

TABLE OF CONTENTS

Chapter 1

Chapter 2

Chapter 3

Nearly There

"There's the lake, Josie," Dad said. "Only ten more minutes now."

Josie frowned and turned her head away. She'd been trying to forget that they were going waterskiing. Instead, she tried to think about seeing Lena again. But it was hard. Dad had so many stories about waterskiing with Steve in the 'old days.'

Dad and Steve had worked together years ago. When Dad moved to the city, they had kept in touch. Steve and his kids, Carlo and Lena, came to the city every year to visit. This was only the second time in 15 years that they had visited Steve at the lake.

The water looked calm, but Josie wasn't
fooled. She knew that if she tried to
water-ski on this water, she'd sink
straight into the slimy mud on the
bottom. Just like last time!

Their boat was the first one on the lake. Steve said that within an hour there could be as many as 20 boats, all dropping off and picking up skiers. This tiny stretch of beach looked too small for more than one or two boats.

"Don't they crash into each other?" Josie asked.

"Not very often," said Steve. "If everyone follows the rules, then everyone's safe." He listed a million rules, finishing with, ". . . but there's only one you really need to remember. If you fall, put one hand up in the air. Then everyone can see you, and you'll be safe."

"Safe!" thought Josie. "It doesn't sound safe to me. Staying onshore—that's safe."

Last year was the only other time Josie had tried to water-ski. The boat had started and stopped, started and stopped, circling around her. They had to bring the rope back to her every time she fell off, which was all of the time.

Finally, when even Lena had run out of helpful hints, Josie had managed to stand, wobbling, on those slippery skis. She stood for three whole seconds! But in the fourth second, she fell.

She had clung to the rope and was
dragged along under the murky water.
Slimy weeds brushed across her face and
grabbed at her legs. By the time the rope
was pulled from her hands, she'd gulped
enough water to fill a fishbowl.

Then she vomited and vomited. They had
to go home. Dad hadn't been skiing for
years, and he didn't even get a chance
that day. Dad was quiet all the way
home, making Josie feel even worse.

He still talked about it and made jokes, but Josie couldn't laugh. Dad had waited for so long, and she'd ruined it for him.

CHAPTER 2

It Looks So Simple

"Come on the boat, Josie," Dad called.

"I'll just watch," Josie answered.

She didn't want to go near the water. It was full of mud, weeds, and things with claws, hiding in the mud. Josie was a good swimmer, but she liked to be able to see the bottom. There was no way she was going into this water.

Dad shrugged. It was easy for him. He was good at everything. Why couldn't he see that it wasn't so easy for her? Josie wished she had stayed home. But then she wouldn't have seen Lena.

Dad pushed the boat out into deeper water, then jumped in with Lena and Steve. Carlo was floating in the water, ready for his turn. Lena threw the towrope to him. He grabbed the handle, and the boat started moving. When the rope was taut, the engine roared and they took off.

Carlo seemed to just pop out of the
water, up onto the one ski. They headed
around the lake, Carlo zigzagging behind
the boat. He sent up a wall of spray as
he turned. Josie watched as the boat
shrank into the distance.

After a while, the boat came back. As it got closer, it headed straight toward the beach. It zoomed past Josie as it turned. Carlo dropped the rope and glided in toward shore.

"Just my luck," he said. "I wanted to ski onto the shore!" He slapped his hand down on the water. "I'll do it next time."

Now it was Lena's turn. Carlo slid the ski out to her. She jumped into the water and spent a minute adjusting the foot binding. As the boat came around, she grabbed the rope, then gave the thumbs-up sign. Lena popped out of the water as soon as the boat took off. As she turned, she made water sprays that were even bigger than Carlo's.

It wasn't fair. They made it look so easy.
Couldn't they try to make it look a little
bit hard? Then Josie might not feel so
bad. She didn't care if she couldn't make
sprays like Carlo and Lena. Josie just
wanted to be able to stand up on the skis.

The boat turned. Josie's heart began to
thump. She was running out of excuses.

The boat sped straight for shore, turning at the last moment. Lena let go of the rope and started to slow down. As she bobbed in the water, she removed her ski. She walked out of the water laughing.

"Your turn, Josie," said Dad. He was holding up a wet suit and a life jacket.

CHAPTER 3

Dad's Turn

"NO! Oh, no thanks, Dad. It's okay. Maybe later. You go first . . ."

Dad turned away. She could tell he was disappointed. Josie was hoping that they'd run out of time, or maybe gas. Then she wouldn't look so hopeless.

"You should try it, Josie. It's fun," Lena
said. "Everyone is scared at first. I was
shaking so much before my first time, I
could hardly get my gear on!"

Josie stared at Lena. It was hard to
imagine Lena being scared. She always
looked so relaxed. Josie looked at her
own hands. At least they weren't shaking.

"Are you sure you don't want a turn,
Josie?" Steve asked.

Josie hesitated. Maybe it would be okay.
Maybe this time would be different. She
started to speak, but Steve was looking at
her dad. Josie felt ashamed.

"Looks like it's your turn, Pete," said
Steve. "This should be a laugh."

Dad put on a life jacket. He was already wearing his old wet-suit pants. Dad said they used to be green and navy blue. They had faded to different shades of gray, and the stitching was fraying.

It must be nearly 15 years since Dad has been waterskiing, Josie was thinking. What if he's forgotten how to ski? This could be embarrassing—even more embarrassing than those wet-suit pants. But if Dad fell, it might make him think. He might begin to know how she felt.

"C'mon, Pete. Let's see if you can still get out of the water!" Steve called.

Dad put the ski on. Lena threw the rope to him. Steve idled the boat to take up the slack in the rope. Dad wobbled a little in the water, trying to get himself straight. He gave the thumbs-up sign and the boat took off. So did Dad—straight up and then over—flat on his face! He came up spluttering and coughing. Josie smiled grimly. Good! It was his turn.

Josie sat down on her towel at the edge of the beach. She watched as Steve turned the boat and circled back so Dad could pick up the rope. This time, Dad got up on the ski. At first he was stiff and awkward. Then he started to have fun. By the time he was at the halfway point, he was crossing the lake from side to side.

He fell off once on the other side of the lake, and it took several tries before he could get up. This time he skied right behind the boat and didn't try anything fancy. When the boat came back to the beach, Dad tried to glide in, but ended up falling face-first again. He came up frowning.

"I used to be able to coast in every time.
I never fell." He stood up, then groaned
and rubbed his shoulder.

"You're getting too old for this," laughed
Steve from the boat. "We'll have to put
you back on two skis!"

Dad's face darkened. "Maybe." He
dumped the ski on the sand and climbed
back into the boat. "It's your turn, Josie,"
he yelled.

Lena came and sat down next to Josie.

Lena Understands

"Just try, Josie. If you fall, the life jacket will hold you up. Just make sure you let go of the rope," said Lena.

Josie took a deep breath. "But I don't know how," she whispered.

"The first time is the hardest," said Lena.

Josie agreed with that. Nothing could be as bad as last time.

"And the worst part is that you think you are wasting everyone's time," Lena added.

Lena was saying what Josie was thinking. She understood. How come Dad didn't?

Lena continued, "My dad loves teaching people to ski." She rolled her eyes. "He never stops. He gets you up on two skis first, then one. Then he teaches you tricks. Every time I start to relax, he thinks he has to teach me something new, and it's always hard."

Josie looked over at the two dads laughing together. She started to think that maybe all dads were the same. They all pushed their kids.

"Come on, try it," said Lena.

"I guess . . ." said Josie. She took the gear and put it on while Lena got the two skis for her.

As they waded out together, Josie held her breath. As soon as the water was deep enough, Josie leaned back and let the vest keep her afloat. Lena helped steady her while Josie put on the skis.

Josie could feel a thumping in her chest. Thrills swept out to her fingers and toes, then returned to jiggle in her stomach.

Steve yelled from the boat as it cruised
past, "Curl your body up into a ball, lean
back, and let the boat do the work."

Lena touched Josie's shoulder. "Stay curled
up tight with the skis in front of you.
You'll be fine. Tell me when you're ready."

Ready? She'd never be ready. Why couldn't it be something that she was good at? An image of last time flashed into her head. She blinked rapidly, chasing away the memory of rushing water, slimy weeds, and vomit. What was she doing here?

Lena looked at her, eyebrows raised. Josie only nodded, but she really wanted to say, "No! No! Never!" Lena gave Steve the thumbs-up sign.

CHAPTER 5

Water Is for Fish

The boat revved and Josie felt the water pressing against the bottom of the skis. She pushed her feet hard against the skis and felt herself rising through the water. Maybe she could do it.

Her skis tipped to one side, and she went underwater! The rope was pulled from her hands. She bobbed back up. Lena was there before she stopped coughing.

That was it! Josie thought. Water was for fish, and she didn't have gills.

"If you lose your balance, let the rope go. If you hold on, you'll just get dragged under. Did you swallow any water?" Lena asked.

Josie realized she hadn't. At least she'd learned one thing from last time.

The boat was coming around again. Lena reached for the rope.

"Look, I'm not so sure . . . ," said Josie. But Lena handed her the rope before she could continue.

"You'll get the hang of it," Lena said.

Easy for her to say. She was probably born with skis on her feet. Josie grinned at the idea of a baby wearing skis.

Lena grinned back. "I know it's hard to believe, but if you relax, it will be easier."

The boat took off again. Twice, Josie went sideways and—splat! The next time, she was almost standing when the skis decided to go in opposite directions. Josie fell flat on her face. She felt really stupid—and embarrassed.

As the boat came back, Josie said, "I'm getting tired. Maybe I should stop."

Steve looked at Josie. "You were so close. Keep your arms bent until you're up. When you get out of the water, keep your knees bent and your back straight."

How was she supposed to remember all that? This bent, that straight. It was all so strange and difficult.

She lay back, letting the life jacket support her. Knees bent, arms bent, lean back. Okay. Last try. If she goofed this time, she'd give up. She'd probably never get it. Some people probably never could do it. Or worse—maybe she was the first one! Maybe she was just hopeless.

CHAPTER 6

One More Try

Josie gave the thumbs-up sign. The boat sped up. She held the rope and got ready for the pull on her arms. It came and pulled her through the water, then up.

Up! She was up! On top of the water.
Moving. Arms bent. No, legs bent. No,
knees bent, back straight, arms straight.
Arms straight? Oh, no!

Josie felt the rope go slack. She pulled on the rope, bending her arms even more. The next thing she knew, she was back in the water, and the skis were no longer on her feet. One was next to her, and the other one was floating away.

She floated and watched the boat come around. Carlo reached over the side of the boat for the other ski, and it came gliding toward her.

"Josie, that was great! You were up! You did it!" Dad sounded really excited.

Josie began to smile. Maybe she could do it. Maybe she wasn't hopeless after all.

"Try to keep your arms straight. If the rope gets slack, lift it over your head. Don't try to pull it in," said Dad.

Josie nodded. She put the skis back on and grabbed the rope.

The boat pulled her up again. She was up! Josie felt as though she were flying, like she was gliding on top of the water. The water was racing beneath her feet, silky smooth. White froth zoomed away on either side of the skis. She looked at the boat. Dad was waving his arms in the air.

Josie grinned. She watched her skis glide over the water. She leaned to one side, then panicked as she shot over to the edge of the wake. She straightened again and moved, as if by magic, back to the middle.

Josie stayed behind the boat until she began to feel more confident. She leaned just a little bit, moving left, then right, then back to the middle. She began to relax.

Josie looked up to see Carlo and Dad waving at her and pointing at the shore. She could hardly believe she'd made it all the way around. Steve slowed the boat, and Josie let go of the rope.

Lena splash-danced out to her. "Josie! You did it! You did it!"

Josie's grin felt wide enough to split her face. "That was SOOO good! I didn't want to stop!"

Lena laughed. "I knew you'd love it."

The boat coasted in alongside them.

"I knew you could do it," said Dad. "What a star!"

"Yay! Can I have another turn?" asked Josie.

GLOSSARY

adjusting
changing the position

awkward
stiff and clumsy

binding
the part of the ski that
holds the foot

fraying
coming apart at the
seams

hesitated

paused with doubt

idled

moved at the slowest speed

revved

gained power

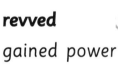

taut

pulled tight

towrope

the rope that the skiers hold onto

Talking with the Author and the Illustrator

Claire Saxby (author)

What do you keep under your bed?
   Socks, in case my feet get cold.

What are you most scared of?
   Running out of time to do/try everything I want
   to do/try.

Sue O'Loughlin (illustrator)

What day of the year do you like best?
   The first day of vacation, before you get bored.

What do you keep under your bed?
   A snack or two, a pet or two, and socks.

What are you most scared of?
   Heights . . . which is really silly because if you
   hang on tight, you're OK.

Published by Sundance Publishing
P.O. Box 1326, 234 Taylor Street, Littleton, MA 01460
800-343-8204
www.sundancepub.com

First published 2000 as Sparklers by
Blake Education, Locked Bag 2022, Glebe 2037, Australia
Exclusive United States Distribution: Sundance Publishing

ISBN 0-7608-6980-4